Adverbially Challenged

Volume 2

Mike's Not-Entirely-Serious Wantonly-Rule-Breaking Adverb Writing Challenge was conceived by Mike Scott Thomson.

First published March 2017.

You can learn more about Mike's Not-Entirely-Serious Wantonly-Rule-Breaking Adverb Writing Challenge and many other writing challenges at:

www.christopherfielden.com

ISBN: 1544051344
ISBN-13: 978-1544051345

DEDICATION

This book is dedicated to all the writers that have contributed stories to Mike's Not-Entirely-Serious Wantonly-Rule-Breaking Adverb Writing Challenge.

Obviously, without you, these books definitely would absolutely not printedly or eBookly exist.

Thanking you all muchly.

Mike Scott Thomson & Chris Fielden

INTRODUCTION 1

by Mike Scott Thomson

To -Ly, or not to -Ly – that is the question
Whether 'tis nobler on the page to suffer
The slings and arrows of outrageous adverbs
Or to take arms against a sea of editors
And by opposing end them....

Well, who knew we'd end up here?

For those thus far unaware, Mike's Not-Entirely-Serious Wantonly-Rule-Breaking Adverb Writing Challenge was conceived as I was writing an article for Chris Fielden's website. I was tackling the thorny subject of those so-called writing 'rules' and that – you know – it may be fun to break them once in a while.

Write a story, maximum 100 words, Chris and I challenged. *Use as many adverbs as you can.*

To our surprise and amusement, we received many entries. To our *pleasant* surprise, these stories were clever, entertaining and often very funny.

Maybe there was indeed something to this whole breaking the 'rules' business.

Now – and welcome, by the way – herewith our second volume of *Adverbially Challenged*, crammed to bursting point with 100 bite-sized stories, heavily featuring this much-maligned grammatical quirk.

But now it may be worth asking: why the adverb? Why is it a writing 'rule' to snip them out as much as possible? They do have their function. Don't they?

To my mind, the use of adverbs (alongside adjectives, exclamation marks, flat verbs, and all these other apparent literary no-no's) are typically tools of 'telling'. The guidance writers are always given is that better practice is to 'show'. Indeed, 'show, don't tell' has been imparted so frequently down the years that it has itself turned into a bit of a literary cliché.

Personally, I don't think good creative writing can ever be quite as simple as 'show' being good, 'tell' being bad. For me, it comes down to the demands and pacing of the story you're writing. Each story will have its own ratio of 'show' to 'tell'. It's impossible to have, to almost coin a phrase, 'one rule to ring them all'.

But how does the writer decide which parts of a story should be a 'show' and which parts, if any, need to be zipped along with a straightforward, no-frills 'tell' – including, maybe, the use of some selective adverbs, if the meaning behind them is vital to the narrative and the same meaning hasn't already been implied by the context?

That, indeed, is the question.

I use the odd adverb in my stories – admittedly, less now than I used to (largely thanks to having weaned myself off them via the partaking of my own challenge). I find if I search my first draft for elements like adverbs, and other tools of 'telling' like exclamation marks or adjectives, the yellow-highlighted result can be a very handy way of determining whether a story has the right balance of show-to-tell. How many are there, should there be that many and, if so, are they in the right places?

The late, great Terry Pratchett once said, "The first draft is just you telling yourself the story." So I would make a bold suggestion: use all these tools of 'telling' like adverbs, exclamation marks etc., as much as you like when, as Sir Terry says, you're 'telling' yourself the story. That will give you something to work with when editing and rewriting away. And who knows, you may even decide to leave in one or two of the first-draft adverbs in the final version. For all the writing 'rules', for all these 'best practice' guidelines and 'show, don't tells', an occasional, well-placed adverb – if it truly earns its place – can make a difference.

As, I hope, we can see in this adverb-crammed, wantonly-rule-breaking book you're holding now. And it's for charity, too. Who's to argue with that?

Finally, thanks to all those who have supported my daft challenge by either contributing stories, or by buying the books – I hope you enjoy this one.

To read, perchance to dream…

INTRODUCTION 2

by Chris Fielden

When Mike and I started this challenge, we wondered if we'd get to 20 submissions. At the time of writing this introduction, we've received 227 stories. The generosity of the writing community never ceases to amaze me.

I'd like to say a huge thank you to everyone that's submitted their work to the Adverb Challenge and to everyone who has purchased our anthologies. Without you, none of this would be possible.

I thought it would be nice to share a quick history of the Adverb Challenge and how it's developed over time as part of this introduction.

Mike's Not-Entirely-Serious Wantonly-Rule-Breaking Adverb Writing Challenge was first launched in April 2016 when Mike wrote a post for my website. You can read said post here:

www.christopherfielden.com/short-stories/me-robot-by-mike-scott-thomson.php

On 24th June 2016, we received our 20th submission, so we created a dedicated page on my website for the challenge.

On 3rd August 2016, we received our 100th story. We also received our 101st submission. It's by Allen Ashley and is entitled 'The Final Word'.

Here are some words that appear on the site, inspired by Allen's beautifully failed attempt to clinch spot 100 in *Adverbially Challenged Volume 1*:

An opening note from Chris Fielden.

Sadly, the legendary Allen Ashley regrettably missed out on the deliciously tempting target of submitting story number 100 to the Adverb Challenge. Ironically, his

delightfully entitled story will open Adverbially Challenged Volume 2. *Somehow, I feel this is fitting for this splendidly silly test of tantalisingly titillating adverb usage.*

And from Mike Scott Thomson:

So, we made it to 100 (and beyond). Thanks so much to everyone for contributing to this undoubtedly daft, but indubitably satisfying challenge – and I'm sure First Story will be pleased too. Very much looking forward to Adverbially Challenged Volume 1 *being released in November, just in time – hopefully – for the filling of stockings (Yulely).*

And as for Volume 2, *in the spirit of wantonly-rule-breaking, I couldn't think of a more appropriate story to kick things off than one called 'The Final Word'. Verily, I see great things ahead.*

In November 2016, *Adverbially Challenged Volume 1* was released. We sold quite a few copies on the run up to Christmas and made our first donation to First Story, the charity the challenge supports, in January 2017. The book continues to sell a few copies every month. To date, we have raised £108 for charity.

On 26th January 2017 we received our 200th submission. *Adverbially Challenged Volume 2* was released in March 2017. We're hoping the launch of this book will mean we sell more copies of the first anthology, along with a plethora of copies of this book, meaning even more money can be donated to First Story.

This is all from just one writing challenge.

At the time of writing, there are two more challenges running on my website:

1. Lesley's Nifty Nib-Nibbling Nonsensical Narrative Writing Challenge

2. Allen's Sensory Overload Writing Challenge

In June 2017 I'll be launching Chris's Colossal Cliché Count Writing Challenge in conjunction with the Bath Flash Fiction Festival. You can learn more about that here:

www.flashfictionfestival.com

I hope that over time the writing challenges will generate £1,000s for charity and result in 1,000s of authors being published. As time goes on, this vision becomes more and more likely. Thank you all for helping me make a (rather crazy) dream become reality.

Stories in this book start at number 101 and go up to 200. You can read stories 1 to 100 in *Adverbially Challenged Volume 1*.

I hope you enjoy the entertaining stories contained within this glorious tome of wonderment.

Over and out.

INTRODUCTION 3

by First Story

First Story changes lives through writing. We believe that writing can transform lives, and that there is dignity and power in every young person's story.

First Story brings talented, professional writers into secondary schools serving low-income communities to work with teachers and students to foster creativity and communication skills. By helping students find their voices through intensive, fun programmes, First Story raises aspirations and gives students the skills and confidence to achieve them.

We are so thrilled and grateful for the support of the editors, authors and readers of this anthology; you are helping to nurture the talent, creativity and confidence of young writers from across the UK.

ACKNOWLEDGMENTS

Big thanks to Mike Scott Thomson for conceiving and helping me bring the Adverb Challenge to life. You can learn more about Mike on his website: www.mikescottthomson.com

Thanks to David Fielden for designing the cover of this book and building and maintaining my website. Without him, I'd never have created a platform that allowed the writing challenges I run to be so successful. You can learn more about Dave's website building skills at: www.bluetree.co.uk

And finally, a HUMONGOUS thank you to everyone who has submitted stories, purchased anthologies and supported this crazy idea and, in turn, the First Story charity. At the time of writing, we are already over a quarter of the way to 100 submissions for *Adverbially Challenged Volume 3*. Without the support and generosity of all the writers who submit their stories and readers who buy the anthologies, this simply wouldn't be possible. You're all totally amazing.

ADVERBIALLY CHALLENGED

101: THE FINAL WORD

by Allen Ashley

In the nick of time, I roused myself slowly and sullenly, complete with a good talking-to, knowing instinctively that the job would never get done if I simply passed my days lazily and carelessly or instead left the task to be completed finally by one of my peer group when instead it behoved me to focus diligently and claim the last spot which I would make rightfully mine even if what I had to say had been said better and more succinctly and intelligently long before my time in the spotlight that lingered briefly. Spot 100 would be mine. Totally.

~

Allen Ashley's Biography

Allen Ashley: award-winning editor, writer and poet. He works as a creative writing tutor with five groups running across north London. His most recent book is an updated version of his novel *The Planet Suite* (Eibonvale press, 2016).

www.allenashley.com

102: CLENCH

by Mel Ciavucco

I tightly hold in the bubbles of air annoyingly edging through my rectum. *Not in downward dog in a full yoga class*, I think, nervously.

Anxiously, I wonder if maybe I can unobtrusively slip it out. Just a little whoosh, inconspicuously.

I very slightly release my clench. Steadily, gradually, slowly. And unintentionally let out an enormously huge fart.

Everyone's obviously silently disgusted.

We're coyly moving through another round of sun salutations quietly. Then we're in downward dog again, and suddenly – another fart. This time, not me. Perfectly and loudly rumbly, beautifully ringing in my ears, I happily come to standing.

~

Mel Ciavucco's Biography

Mel Ciavucco is a Bristol based writer and podcaster. She writes novels, screenplays, short stories – anything from gritty drama to gross-out zombie comedy – and blogs about gender equality.

www.melciavucco.weebly.com

103: PROSPECTS

by Mark Rutterford

Jonno confidently walked towards Safia. He falteringly asked her out.

Unequivocally, Safia said, "No."

Jonno made the toe-curlingly embarrassing walk back to the bar. He hastily downed a glass of beer and energetically downed another.

Jonno drunkenly resolved to not take 'no' for an answer.

Safia patiently waited.

Jonno teeteringly swayed towards Safia, irresponsibly waving yet another glass of ale before him.

Safia, pre-emptively and forcefully, shook her head.

Jonno, balletically pirouetted and then unstably pirouetted and then ill-advisedly pirouetted some more. Jonno spectacularly fell to the floor and refreshingly bathed in his spilt drink.

Safia enigmatically smiled. Jonno too.

~

Mark Rutterford's Biography

Mark Rutterford writes and performs his stories in the towns and cities of South West England.

If you see him reading live, he is likely to have a prop in his hand and a heart on his sleeve.

www.markrutterford.com

104: SCINTILLATINGLY DELIVERED

by Michael Rumsey

He'd waited anxiously to hear from his normally actively and engagingly helpful agent and now a glorious glittering opportunity for an ambitiously minded aspiring actor had arisen.

Painstakingly, he'd written a dazzlingly attractive script. He'd patiently and studiously practiced making hand gestures flourishingly sincere while skillfully controlling breathing in order to emphatically produce every syllable accordingly.

Brightly, confidently he stepped into the Casting Director's splendidly furnished office and began his sparkling speech.

"Refreshingly, eloquently, cleverly delivered," she acknowledged as he brilliantly ended a positively glorious audition, "but the part we are casting is that of a deaf mute unfortunately."

~

Michael Rumsey's Biography

Michael lives in Athens with wife Maria, dog Sammy, several Greek Tax Demands and a laptop that just occasionally does as it is told.

105: CHOCOLATE DELIGHT

by June Whitaker

Obviously, driving one-handedly, albeit unhurriedly, while pleasurably licking a Double Choc Delight on a sizzlingly hot day could regrettably earn me a toe-curlingly painful fine. I've already hastily but reluctantly thrown it to the floor, but the policeman officiously stops me.

"What's wrong, Officer?" I querulously ask, while winsomely fluttering my eyelashes and desperately wishing I were 20 or, preferably, 40 years younger.

He purposefully lifts his sunglasses and lecherously ogles my cleavage. "Drive carefully, Grandma," he growls, casually waving me on.

My sundress clings uncomfortably. Briefly glancing down, I see I've incriminatingly dribbled Choc Delight. So embarrassingly geriatric.

~

June Whitaker's Biography

British expat living in Spain. Sun worshipper – surprise, surprise – keen gardener and walker, doting granny, among many astounding attributes. Also unpublished novelist (living in hope).

www.junewhitaker.es

106: GOING FOR GOLD

by Allen Ashley

Suddenly inspired childishly.
Back lawn re-enactment Olympically.
Running and jumping breathlessly.
Wishing and dreaming tentatively.
Outlasting classmates classily.
Focused on fitness physically.
Attending trials hopefully.
Winning contests joyously.
Being coached regularly.
Training daily and rigorously.
Starting to improve noticeably.
Setting personal bests frequently.
Lagging at top level nationally.
Considering approaches tactically.
Seeking advantage surreptitiously.
Bending the rules covertly.
Supplementing diet miraculously.
Making great strides suddenly.
Seen to achieve visibly.
Hauling in medals greedily.
Progress considered questionably.
Investigations conducted thoroughly.
Reputation tarnished permanently.
Facing the music dopily.
Struck from the record books shamefully.

~

Allen Ashley's Biography

See story 101.

107: GIVE A BAG A SECOND CHANCE

by J. Rosina Harlow

There is, undoubtedly, life beyond one fleeting, obligatory, hasty trip to the gargantuan supermarket.

Fresh and feisty, you unfurled joyfully and selflessly accepted the heavy tins.

Now you lie, regretfully, scrunched forgetfully into the corner of the capacious boot of a shiny car.

You had thought, foolishly, that a bag might be for life, but for whatever flimsy, insubstantial, thin and easily torn reason, you are lonely, neglected, unloved.

You wish fervently that someone would kindly adopt you, oh misunderstood plastic miracle, to let you tumble and fly with your cellophane friends across their unspoilt and verdant gardens, forever.

~

J. Rosina Harlow's Biography

J. Rosina Harlow graduated from University College Chichester in 2005 as a joint recipient of the Philip Le Brun Prize for Creative Writing.

She writes dark and surreal short stories.

A Kent based musician, she is married, with three cats.

www.facebook.com/JRosinaHarlow

108: THE ESCAPE

by Joan Withington

She gingerly made her way to the front door. Annoyingly, it was locked.

Falteringly retracing her steps, she suddenly leapt up the stairs. She hurriedly made her way along the landing. Surprisingly and quite unexpectedly, the bathroom door was invitingly open. She crept in. The smell of perfume hung in the air, overwhelmingly revolting and powerfully pungent. It filled her lungs. She felt sick.

Her pathetically highly pitched meows failed to attract anyone's attention so she had no option but to bravely leap through the window on to the invitingly low branches of the stunningly blossoming pear tree.

~

Joan Withington's Biography

No author biography supplied.

109: HOMECOMING

by Alex Wilson

I always hear him come home. The front door bangs loudly, angrily. I hide under the duvet shivering quietly, breathing rapidly, lying rigidly. I imagine him stumbling blindly, recklessly in the kitchen. My heart thumps frantically.

Carelessly I have left Bear somewhere. I want him desperately, but more than that, I want to be elsewhere, anywhere. I hate the nightly hands roughly coaxing me to behave reluctantly but obediently.

The bedroom door opens quietly. Foolishly I move. Numbly I wait.

He speaks softly, "Are you going to be friendly tonight? Daddy's home."

~

Alex Wilson's Biography

No author biography supplied.

110: THE GIG WAS UP

by Diane Caldwell

She stepped quietly, carefully, trying desperately to be utterly silent. Each step landed stealthily as a totally absorbed cat slowly stalking its completely unaware prey.

She instinctively knew that absolutely everything depended wholeheartedly on her ability to unabashedly surprise her victim. She silently crept up step by step, holding her breath, intrinsically using the martial arts skills she so painstakingly developed. And then suddenly and utterly unexpectedly her quarry turned screaming piercingly, like an extremely over-excited rooster, rapidly flailing her arms higgledy-piggledy, and excitedly kicking her legs about like a high-steppin' cakewalker.

She knew then, unmistakably, the gig was up.

~

Diane Caldwell's Biography

14 years ago, stifling sobs, Diane Caldwell boarded a plane and left the US. Currently she rents a room in Goa, India where she dances like a banshee at the sunset drum circle, watches sea eagles soar over the jungle and writes when the muse whispers.

www.adventuresinarambol.blogspot.com

111: HIGH FLYER

by Joan Withington

Like a bird of prey, slowly, silently and serenely the tiny plane cruised high in the cerulean sky.

Unexpectedly, a seemingly badly timed turn sent it plunging towards the mountains, downwardly spiraling in a dizzyingly, dangerously dramatic dance.

Wide eyed, I held my breath, fearfully anticipating a potentially disastrous ending.

Suddenly I heard an expertly engineered full throttling of the engine. Abruptly the plane levelled out and quietly disappeared from view over the snowcapped peaks.

I realised, alarmingly, I had developed cramp in my neck and, unfortunately, I could no longer look down at my skis.

Help.

~

Joan Withington's Biography

See story 108.

112: MINUS FIVE

by Jerry Wilson

"Dad," Hopefully whined, annoyedly. "Loudly's name was tastelessly included in Chris's wildly successful adverb anthology. Why wasn't my name respectfully mentioned?"

"Son, I've recently been meaning to tell you, although reluctantly," his father, Stoically, sighed remorsefully. "We're nouns. Loudly, regrettably has no cause to confidently crow. He's a noun, too."

"What? Are adverbs unreasonably deemed better than we judiciously and properly used nouns?"

"To people like the estimably regarded Chris, they assuredly are," Stoically said, facetiously.

"Why did our author use our names, then, if adverbs didn't really count?"

"He muddle-headedly assumed that we were adverbs."

~

Jerry Wilson's Biography

An old new writer who, though lacking the talent and imagination of experienced story writers, bows to no one when penning cunning excuses for failed submissions. I fear no adverb. They are but tools in my arsenal of wearisome words.

113: DIY

by Joan Withington

He cautiously prised open the large pot of paint. Disappointingly, there was an oily yellow slick lying supinely on the surface. He gently poked it with a spoon to reveal the astonishingly whiter than white colour beneath.

Breathing a sigh of relief he swiftly stirred the buttercup oily slick into the depths of the pot. Unfortunately, the enthusiastically delivered movement was overwhelmingly over the top. Literally.

Slurping and sloshing over the rim of the can, the paint, tantalisingly and tauntingly flowing like lava, crept onto the kitchen table and slowly, downwardly onto his left foot.

~

Joan Withington's Biography

See story 108.

114: HE WAS THERE

by Tracey Maitland

She sat patiently, stirring her cup of tea. As she methodically, rhythmically pushed the teaspoon around the teacup, she deliciously devoured the thought of seeing him again.

She thought longingly of his eyes, beautifully framed by wonderfully long eyelashes. The contour of his lips lovingly shaped like those of a cherub. As she remembered his kiss, the teaspoon whirled around the agreeably melodic teacup evermore rapidly and her body tingled with an anticipated passion.

She closed her heavily made-up eyes to savour the rapturously remembered moment. The silver teaspoon suddenly missed a circuit around the teacup. He was there.

~

Tracey Maitland's Biography

No author biography supplied.

115: SPEAKING FROM THE HEART

by John Notley

"However," said the Chairman cheerfully, even boyishly, launching his annual speech, "I can happily inform you confidentially," eyes glinting roguishly, "this has been financially, our best year ever. Moreover, undeniably by unstintingly and loyally supporting me, we eventually, admittedly barely, exceeded our target. I can reliably notify you that you will be amply rewarded accordingly."

After listening patiently for two hours to the Chairman's verbosity, Frank the Sales Manager pleadingly raised his eyes upwardly, gratefully and thankfully aware that the end was nigh. "God Bless the Chairman." At which the Chairman clutched his heart and sank gracefully to the floor.

~

John Notley's Biography

John, a retired travel agent, having failed to make his fortune, has taken up his pen again hoping to redress the situation. He had a few stories and poems published some years ago but feels it's time to hit the jackpot.

www.linkedin.com/in/john-notley-503666102/

116: SO HOW NOW

by Rebecca Henderson

Well, probably when we're still there we'll also definitely never again really be going to that place.

Today we went, but not for long. After all, it's perhaps a little childish. Maybe we actually mean the best. Sometimes, of course, everyone has to be a tiny bit of a kid. It's always better to be rather goofy than particularly gruff.

Eventually the world, indeed life, will inevitably catch up. Before then, however, before suddenly and irrevocably snuffing out, we certainly wish to finally mean something. Or, quite simply, nearly change the world around us.

Together, it is enough.

~

Rebecca Henderson's Biography

Rebecca Henderson holds a degree in both German and Creative Writing. She hopes to shift your world perspective through her words, because looking out of the same window every day hardly makes for an interesting life.

www.linkedin.com/in/rebecca-henderson

117: CAKES

by Mike Scott Thomson

The neatherd's wife dutifully attends the cattle whilst The Great King – anonymously, surreptitiously – refuges cosily in her cottage.

Hotly the flames flicker. Dimly he watches the dough rise, anxiously evaluating how history will immortalise him. Famously formidable, or infamously ineffectual?

Aggressively the invaders advance, a rash across the shires. His next course of action shall – crucially, decisively – determine what thusly befalls.

The loaves rapidly blacken as the neatherd's wife returns. Angrily she admonishes, "Thou half-witted knave – to err the simplest of tasks."

"I apologise fulsomely," he replies remorsefully, furiously fanning the fumes, yet assumes – erroneously – this mishap hath no import.

~

Mike Scott Thomson's Biography

Mike Scott Thomson's short stories have been published by journals, anthologies and have won the occasional award, including first prize in Chris Fielden's inaugural To Hull & Back competition.

Based in south London, he works in broadcasting.

www.mikescottthomson.com

118: MISSING THE POINT

by Peter Collins

Earnestly, eloquently (and perhaps even egotistically), I was explaining to Lucy, my lamentably literal life-partner, about my elegantly effective entry to the Adverb Challenge. She was undeniably unimpressed.

"Add verbs," she cheekily chortled. "A child could do it. Freeze and frame equals freeze-frame. Flash and flood equals flash-flood."

"That's not quite how it works..."

My ineffective intervention was imperiously ignored.

"Jump-suit; drink-drive; train-ride..." and on and on and on for the rest of the distressingly distraught-filled day.

~

Peter Collins' Biography

Peter's stories have been featured in anthologies such as *Voices in the Dark* from Bookers Corner, and *Disorderly Lives* published by Writers' Notebook. He is currently looking for an agent to promote his whodunit novel, *Captain Goodheart Investigates*.

119: IT'S FUNNY HOW THESE THINGS COME ABOUT

by J. Rosina Harlow

Tremulously, Mike turned the cold metal torch in his hands and waited expectantly for the familiar strobing signal.

From the starless black sky came brilliant bolts of light, blinking fiercely in rapid, seemingly random, patterns.

The night split thunderously and the air rippled, softly.

"What do you want me to do?" Mike asked, hoarsely.

The answer came presently, conveyed telepathically as he lay nervously back in his warm bed.

The tall one moved forward imperiously and blinked its almond shaped eyes thoughtfully. Then the bulbous grey head began to pulse, ominously.

"You must instigate the adverb challenge," it replied, inscrutably.

~

J. Rosina Harlow's Biography

See story 107.

120: NEW BEGINNINGS

by Judith Wolfgang

I am lovingly thankful for new beginnings. I have always loved writing and now, a little at a time, I'm faithfully writing more and more. Parts of speech used outside of English 101 are exciting and positively delightful.

Many are the varied kindly helpful people who successfully decide to encourage and help new writers.

New beginnings are made with the first step, however slowly made. Who knew that those parts of speech so tedious and challenging would safely guide us on new and exciting paths?

New ideas and bettering our world can be particularly helpful in undertaking new beginnings.

~

Judith Wolfgang's Biography

Judith Wolfgang is a beginning writer who likes simplicity and beauty. She enjoys family, travel and supplying her homemade cookies to her loyal friends and co-workers. The printed work has a magical quality about it. Blessings upon all heart-felt writing.

121: GHOSTLY, TICKLY FINGERS

by Christopher Fielden

"Tickly wickly woo."

"I beg your pardon?" said Maud, ill-temperedly.

"Tickly wickly woooooo," said the ethereally wispy apparition as its ghostly, tickly fingers sneakily snuck into Maud's armpit.

"Stop it immediately, Harold." Being rudely awakened in the incredibly early hours absolutely definitely annoyed Maud deeply. "You know I can't feel a thing and your 'wooing' is... frankly, it's absurdly irritating."

Dejectedly, Harold stopped. "Terribly sorry, dear. Being deceased is deadly boring."

"When you're being despicably haunted by your decidedly dead husband, being alive is doubtlessly worse."

"Goodbye, dear, permanently."

"Irrevocably?"

"Decidedly."

"Finally." Maud went to sleep, rapidly.

~

Christopher Fielden's Biography

Chris writes, runs a humorous short story competition, plays drums and rides his motorcycle, sometimes to Hull. And back again.

He has recently started running writing challenges and hopes to publish 1,000s of authors in the support of

charity.
www.christopherfielden.com

122: SECOND

by Judith Wolfgang

It was my second attempt at making that angel food cake that looked so good in the cookbook. I wanted to faithfully and lovingly give a beautiful birthday cake to my mother. I hesitantly threw all the batter into the garbage because I had put in salt instead of sugar and it could not be lovingly saved, even for the kindest of mothers. So, on to my third lovingly-crafted baking attempt.

Mothers are so special and kind. This angel food cake for my mother had to be perfect. I would faithfully try again.

~

Judith Wolfgang's Biography

See story 120.

123: PREJUDICIOUSLY PROUD

by Ros Byrne

Mr Bingley, wealthily, and Mr Darcy, proudly, ride into Netherfield. The news rapidly reaches shabbily chic Longbourn, where Mr and Mrs Bennet react neglectfully and rose-coloured spectacledly respectively, the girls embroidering tiresomely. Mr Bingley unerringly admires Jane as she dances beautifully while Mr Darcy is condescendingly unimpressed as Lydia carries on sluttishly; Mary embarrassingly and Mrs B ridiculously.

Add wickedly deceiving Wickham and self-importantly pedantic Collins obsequiously venerating the haughtily horrible Lady Catherine and the plot thickens complicatedly.

Eventually Elizabeth topples Darcy from his ungentlemanly high horse directly to the altar and they all reside happily ever after.

~

Ros Byrne's Biography

No author biography supplied.

124: WHAT NEXT?

by Judith Wolfgang

It is good to get up every morning and wonder what exciting adventure might be available for the day. Isn't that what children lovingly do – look at each day as an exciting adventure?

A chance to thoughtfully sell lemonade for a worthy cause, always with kindness and consideration for your thirsty customer? Willingly help Mum or Dad with their many household chores?

Our loyalty and dedication to being as humbly receptive to life as children is important. To embrace life as the gift that it is. And ask ourselves, what is actually next in my life?

~

Judith Wolfgang's Biography

See story 120.

125: FRUSTRATED FROLICS

by Lesley Truchet

Feeling fiercely frisky, I prepared punctiliously, patting my pulse spots with a profuse patina of perfume. I carefully clothed myself in a scarlet skirt, fastidiously fabricated to scarcely secrete my charming confidentials and mischievously matched it with a skin-tight see-through top.

Bereft of a brassiere and briefs, I slipped on some sensual stockings and suspenders and roguishly released my tawny tresses. I winkled out a whip from the toy trunk and cracked it carnally as I jumped jauntily on to the bed, waking my weary wonder boy.

He fuzzily focused, muttered, "Oh my God," and callously continued to snore sonorously.

~

Lesley Truchet's Biography

Lesley Truchet has been writing for several years and has a number of short stories, articles and poetry published on paper and on the internet. She is currently writing her first novel.

126: IMPERFECTLY LAUNCHED

by S.B. Borgersen

Freshly published colourfully jacketed novels were totteringly stacked ready for the ferociously advertised launch, the author deliberately positioned for the precisely timed reading.

In the shufflingly slow line-up, Fiona opened her copy excitedly, hopefully, to find it shockingly, horrendously peppered liberally with adverbs.

Exasperatingly, screwing her puckeringly pretty face, gritting perfectly pearly-white teeth, she unwittingly muttered, "How can this famously well-published author stupidly think this will be unbeatably successful?"

Hearing her voice, Fiona's slobberingly loving hound, Titus, enthusiastically bounded bouncily to his mistress, sending the precariously balanced book tower multi-directionally across the book shop floor.

~

S.B. Borgersen's Biography

S.B. Borgersen, originally from England, founder of The Liverpool Literary Society, writes, makes music and concocts recipes for doggy cookies, on the shores of Nova Scotia, Canada. Her poetry and short fiction is published internationally in anthologies and literary journals.

www.sueborgersen.com

127: THE REJECTION DIARIES

by Maggie Davies

Excitedly, expectantly, eagerly, I snatch the brown envelope from the doormat with trembling and sweatily nervous fingers. My breath is pounding crazily and my heart racing feverishly in my fluttering chest.

Fumblingly, I ease out my lovingly crafted pages, spread them tenderly on my lap and disbelievingly scan the hurtfully callous words on the carelessly attached compliment slip: REGRETFULLY WE MUST REJECT YOUR SUBMISSION.

Keeningly, savagely, vengefully I screechingly call down curses on the heads of these ignorant twits and their cruel and foolishly short-sighted response.

How can such obviously ignorant brutes stomp so savagely on my hopes?

~

Maggie Davies' Biography

No author biography supplied.

128: THE PHONE AND WIND COINCIDENCE

by Meredith Schulhof

It was a ridiculously windy day outside. I anxiously paced my room waiting for the wind to stop so that I could continually help my best friend with homework. I was hopeful that she was waiting calmly and comfortably. I knew that she would be abnormally mad if I wasn't there soon.

Coincidentally, my phone rang when my mind processed that thought. Instinctively, I picked up the phone. I was sure it would be my friend who was calling me angrily but when I picked up the phone I was bewildered to hear an annoyingly loud advertiser on the phone.

~

Meredith Schulhof's Biography

No author biography supplied.

129: WHAT EVERYONE MUST KNOW ABOUT THE BEAUTIFULLY LIT SKY

by Meredith Schulhof

I was carefully watching the beautifully lit sky to make sure that nothing harmfully passed my view. I had to spend the whole annoyingly long night carefully looking up into the sky full of sparkly stars.

Apparently, I fell asleep under the sky when I was annoyingly shaken roughly. I reluctantly got up. I knew that my friend would yell angrily at me for me being lazily sleeping. Luckily, nothing happened while I was sleepily sleeping the night away.

The next night, the same thing happened and it turned out that the sky was magically making the guard fall asleep.

~

Meredith Schulhof's Biography

See story 128.

130: THE MYSTERIOUS OBJECT

by Meredith Schulhof

The lights suddenly went completely dark and I frightfully waited for the beautifully colourful lights to come back on. I wanted to sneakily continue on my mission. I was supposedly alone but I jumped frightfully when I heard something rustling quietly alongside me.

I carefully took out my obnoxiously big phone. The object was bewildering me by literally and skillfully knowing my next move. There was no hope in unpredictability, so I literally ran as quickly as I could past the object.

I had no hope in outrunning it. It was flying smoothly straight past me to block the entrance.

~

Meredith Schulhof's Biography

See story 128.

131: DELICIOUSLY & OUTRAGEOUSLY OVERWHELMED BY A SIGNIFICANTLY BEAUTIFUL & GLAMOROUS WITCH

by Richard L. Moriarty

I quietly and anxiously awaited her, obediently and coyly leaning awkwardly and nervously against the lavishly and ornately decorated fountain. Fortunately, she dutifully and quite dramatically arrived astride her elegantly designed and magically powered broomstick.

She was alluringly dressed in a sharply and bravely cut, elegantly styled dress. She dismounted gracefully and gleefully, silently and deftly crossed to my side, unexpectedly took my limply dangling hand and vivaciously pulled me wantonly into her embrace.

Innocently, I warmly and excitedly kissed her perfectly formed and beautifully full lips and she obnoxiously and somewhat irritatingly turned me into a grotesquely malformed frog.

~

Richard L. Moriarty's Biography

Richard is a writer and artist. He promotes sustainability and environmental conservation and improved mental and physical health through engagement with nature.

Richard promotes social enterprises, partnership working and solution based agreements to aid small local businesses to thrive.

132: SUMMERY JUSTICE

by John Galloway

It was literally a posing pouch. A barely there token of glossily, iridescent nylon worn to ensure the maximum exposure of his overly pumped body. He flexed his muscles outrageously, bringing coquettish coos from the fawningly fantasising Fräulines watching admiringly.

The other boys watched sulkily, jealously wishing that, as he strutted arrogantly along the searingly hot sidewalk, he would inadvertently catch the sloppily flip-flopping toe of his sandal on the edge of a poorly maintained paving slab and land embarrassingly on his surgically sculpted nose.

They roared victoriously as he carelessly fulfilled their collectively held fantasy.

He skulked off gloweringly.

~

John Galloway's Biography

John lives and works in London. He has had several books and many articles and blogposts published, mainly about education, special needs and technology.

He is working on his first novel, and enjoys writing poems for children.

www.johngallowayltd.com

133: HE MADE ME – HONESTLY

by Richard L. Moriarty

I was writing inadequately but passionately about an intrinsically difficult topic, that I remarkably and sensationally scripted in lavishly, artistically decorated, beautifully, irrationally coloured script.

I decidedly, overwhelmingly, outdid myself with extraordinarily and ridiculously phrased, insignificantly thought through sentences, that unequivocally proved that I am uninspiringly endowed with a remarkably unexplored ability to uncomfortably waffle, which could undoubtedly send any rationally and sanely motivated person to consider me positively and undoubtedly out of my interestingly unexamined, fractionally endowed tiny insignificantly minuscule little brain.

My only vague attempt to rationally and honestly excuse myself – he told me to do it.

~

Richard L. Moriarty's Biography

See story 131.

134: THE UNINTENTIONALLY ABSENTMINDED SHEPHERDESS AND HER MISCHIEVOUSLY HUNGRY SHEEP

by Valerie Griffin

Dreamily, Little Bo Peep herded the woolly sheep safely into the grassy meadow. Unfortunately, she was behaving distractedly and unsuccessfully failed to notice the surprisingly large gap in the quirkily built fence.

Opportunistically and adventurously, the sheep gleefully escaped into the adjoining field where the grass was lushly greener.

Sleepily, Little Bo Peep took a nap, blissfully unaware the sheep were actually gone. When she woke the field was conspicuously absent of sheep. She frantically searched around and saw them greedily eating in the next meadow. Swiftly and successfully, she rounded them up and sheepishly herded the flock back home.

~

Valerie Griffin's Biography

Published short story and flash fiction writer for anthologies and competitions (one winner plus persistent runner up), letters to magazines and articles.

Find Valerie on Twitter: @griffin399

135: VISIONS OF MIDDLE AGE LETHARGY...

by Nige Street

Whilst rigidly supine, horizontally in the confines of the bath – the watery glove snuggly encasing my torso which once was historically and, rightly so, a deliciously blinding vision of all things Godly – I was beginning to softly yet noticeably acquire the annoyingly shapely characteristics of what could describedly be observed as an overly vacuumed and disproportionately sized duvet sealed within a vastly undersized bin liner.

"Welcome, middle age," I churlishly rumbled.

~

Nige Street's Biography

No author biography supplied.

136: DANGEROUSLY DELICIOUS DELICACIES

by Laura Besley

Patrick was walking to work briskly, whistling softly (and not uncharacteristically out of tune). He stopped abruptly at the pristinely clean window of the baker's.

He stared longingly at the beautifully decorated cakes. His perilously rotund stomach began to growl loudly.

Ted the baker, an exceptionally thin man, waved his hands extravagantly and raised his eyebrows invitingly.

Patrick's ridiculously weak resolve crumbled immediately and he pushed open the door forcefully, causing the bell to ring noisily. "Give me a cake," he said, quickly.

"Of course," the baker replied, gratefully.

Patrick smiled widely and announced joyfully, "The diet can start tomorrow."

~

Laura Besley's Biography

Laura Besley mainly writes short stories (some ridiculously short) in the time that her young son is sleeping. She hopes he'll nap until he leaves home. She also teaches English and currently lives in Hong Kong.

137: JAILBREAK

by Frances Leggatt

Eventually, I get my chance. The Jailer is in the doorway of the apartment, chatting interminably with a neighbour. Slipping surreptitiously off the sofa, I saunter casually towards them.

Recklessly, I plunge through her legs. Then I'm racing frantically down the stairs into the hall. Incredibly, the front door is open.

On the street, I look round warily. Cars shoot past threateningly. Instinctively I dart daintily towards a narrow alleyway and – yes, here's a rubbish bag. It's spilling open untidily, and the stench of yesterday's sushi is beckoning me seductively.

~

Frances Leggatt's Biography

No author biography supplied.

138: WORDS FROM MY GURU

by Allen Ashley

Tread the path lightly.
Keep the faith faithfully.
Support your family supportively.
Cherish your friends amicably.
Deal with your demons diabolically.
For we are less than pawns
in a game played cosmologically
and though we try dutifully
to understand the pattern
knowledgeably and empirically,
we are but bubbles of nothingness
dissipating fizzily into the cold,
flat cola-ness of a universe
cooling entropically.
Does the field mouse comprehend
the nature of the quasar?
Not really.
Is the tapeworm distracted
by Freeview television?
Unlikely.
Tread the path blindly and silently
and you shall be rewarded.
Eventually.
Possibly.

~

Allen Ashley's Biography

See story 101.

139: THUS SPAKE ZARA

by Bartle Sawbridge

"Tell me sincerely," Charles said, "are you coolly, dispassionately, going to leave me thus?"

Assertively, emphatically, almost aggressively, Zara replied that she was, finally. Slowly, deliberately, Charles picked the tightly-sealed, recently delivered letter from the stickily crummy, rarely cleaned, tablecloth.

"Divorce papers," said Zara, calmly.

"But why? I have nearly always cared for you attentively," replied Charles, incredulously.

"'Thus', mainly." Zara rose, straight, from her chair, walked directly from the room, rapidly but quietly along the carpeted hall, and closed the front door behind her for the last time, firmly but soberly, just so.

~

Bartle Sawbridge's Biography

Bartle Sawbridge has published a stunningly satirical novel, *A Piece of String*, (Amazon), and short stories, exceptionally well presented but, adverbially, disappointingly deficient.

140: AT HOME, DARKLY

by Linda Tyler

Smiling secretly, she crept silently into the dimly-lit room.

He fidgeted restlessly in the greasily-covered wing-back chair by the flickering firelight, his sparsely-haired head visibly bobbing over the top.

Closing the door quietly behind her, she moved slowly towards him.

Unaware of her presence, he was moodily reading.

Behind the chair, she leant forwards carefully and placed her smoothly-white hands over his eyes. "Guess who?" she said.

Sighing deeply, he put up his own arthritically-gnarled hands to remove hers. "It's you, Madeline," he said sadly to his skittishly-younger wife.

~

Linda Tyler's Biography

Linda Tyler lives in a village on the edge of the Scottish Highlands. She has been published in UK and US magazines and anthologies.

A retired lecturer, she now runs self-catering holiday accommodation and sings in a local choir.

141: HOW DID YOU DO THAT?

by Rebecca Henderson

Lee precariously pilfered the decadently smothered cinnamon bun from the abnormally-shaped window. Bravely, he coolly scampered up a tree, the considerably large bun clenched daintily in his hands. Presently and methodically, Lee lazily licked the exceptionally-iced treat, eyes closing jubilantly.

Ordinarily he would have thoughtfully left a pretty penny, but zealously and recklessly he had snatched up the sweetly-flavoured savoury dessert. Oddly enough, he was consequently licking his fingers of the sticky residue. Fervently he raced down the tree, leaping incredibly from the sugar. Eagerly he bounded towards the window...

She waited, eyebrow arched brutally. “Lee.”

~

Rebecca Henderson’s Biography

See story 116.

142: AT THE DANCE

by Sheila Gray

She gazed speculatively at the dance floor. Would he tentatively ask her to dance? Would she boldly ask him?

Her rose pink shawl was draped loosely round her shoulders in the chill of the October evening. She concentrated avidly, trying to see him among the dancers.

She felt the shawl gently lifted from her from behind and laid softly on the back of her chair. She turned expectantly. He stood beside her, his hand extended invitingly, smiling shyly.

~

Sheila Gray's Biography

Sheila has lived in rural Aberdeenshire for 35 years and loves the freedom and space. She is retired and relishes the time she now has for writing, particularly the challenge of finding a term to use instead of an adverb.

143: A CHRISTMAS MIRACLE

by Deborah Price

Frozen lake in depths of winter, ice white, glistening, beautiful but cold, so very, very cold.

Fox has cubs to feed, late litter, tiny, starving. No choice, she scampers across, skidding wildly, legs askew. Her destination, island of tasty ducks, firm and plump.

Crack. The ice below creaks and groans, merciless. Scared, stops, thinks she's doomed. But no, silvery snout emerges beneath moon's soft glow, shiny scales flop onto glistening glassy surface.

"Take me," fish mouths.

Shocked, Vixen refuses. "No, don't sacrifice yourself."

"It is my choice," says selfless soul. "Live on, feed your hungry cubs and remember me."

~

Deborah Price's Biography

www.baarbaarathesheep.wordpress.com/about/

144: WAITING, WAITING

by Jade Slee

She drummed her fingers impatiently against the table. *No*, she thought dismissively, *I can't check my phone again, it's only been a few seconds since the last time*. But she stared longingly at the blank screen, praying desperately.

Seconds agonisingly turned to minutes, until finally the phone rang loudly. She speedily picked it up.

"Hey, hon," the voice on the other side drawled lazily. "I'm really sorry, but I'm going to be stuck at work for a while. Go ahead without me."

"OK." She hung up reluctantly and looked at the meal she'd painstakingly prepared.

"Happy anniversary," she murmured, tearfully.

~

Jade Slee's Biography

No author biography supplied.

145: HAYLE STONE AND THE SEVEN ADVERBIALLY-CHALLENGED DIMINUTIVES

by Valerie Griffin

Merrily singing a woodland ditty, Hayle Stone and the seven adverbially-challenged diminutives – Hopelessly, Obnoxiously, Unabashedly, Scarily, Queasily, Joshingly and Majestically – squelched wetly along the terribly wet path through the trees.

Majestically knowledgeably led the way whilst Queasily, feeling anxiously poorly as usual, brought up the rear. Eventually, they reached the mine shaft.

Hayle Stone handed out the lovingly prepared lunch boxes which Hopelessly, Obnoxiously, Unabashedly, Scarily, Queasily, Joshingly and Majestically accepted hungrily. Hayle Stone wished them all a wonderfully good day, then set off skippingly to her physically demanding aerobics class.

~

Valerie Griffin's Biography

See story 134.

146: IN WHICH POOH AND PIGLET ARRIVE APPREHENSIVELY AT THE STREAM

by Margaret Edwards

Pooh sighed wearily. "Now for the Adverbial Stepping Stones."

"What?" gasped Piglet anxiously. "You mean those huge, beautiful, shiny stones?"

"No, little numpty," said Pooh smugly. "Not those redundant Adjectival Stones, these Adverbial Ones here. Allow me to demonstrate."

Pooh jumped across boldly but heavily, splashily and, ultimately, utterly soddenly.

"Bother," said Pooh. "You'll need to be brave, tiny Piglet."

Piglet, however, bounced over lightly, nervously, then increasingly gracefully, daringly and confidently until, gloriously triumphant, he soared rapturously onto the bank.

"Hm," said Pooh as he squelched off humiliatedly. "Where's that Christopher-Mike person? I need, expletively, a word with him."

~

Margaret Edwards' Biography

Writer from age seven, until 30-year gap for absorbing family and job. Now work-free and urgently trying to make up for lost time. Minor poetry prizes and publication, now infatuated with the Short Story but still grovelling in shortlist anterooms.

147: THE INTERVIEW

by Sheila Gray

I entered the room timidly, anxiously. The members of the interview panel rose grandly and proffered their hands politely.

"Why do you want this job? What can you bring to this post?" they asked mundanely.

Then, "What is the worst thing that has ever happened to you?" one asked intrusively.

I wavered sorrowfully between the death of my mother when I was 17 and my recent divorce.

"Will you take this job if it's offered to you?" they asked cheerfully.

"No, I won't," I replied unhappily.

~

Sheila Gray's Biography

See story 142.

148: JACK AND JILLY'S GOODLY DEED ENDS DISASTROUSLY

by Valerie Griffin

Jack and Jilly obediently went up the hilly hillside to fetch sparklingly clear water. Gladly, Jack carried the pail as they strolled, seemingly slowly up the terribly rocky, windingly steep path.

At the top, Jack hitched the pail securely before lowering it smoothly into the darkly well. Finally full, Jilly keenly helped Jack turn the handle and they hauled it up easily.

Carrying it between them, they walked meanderingly down the hill. Jack unexpectedly slipped on the loosely lying scree. He fell, hitting his head clumsily.

Unbalanced, Jilly dropped the pail noisily before somersaulting tumblingly down the hilly hillock.

~

Valerie Griffin's Biography

See story 134.

149: THE FORCED LANDING

by Sheila Gray

The light aircraft flew serenely over the countryside, the engine throbbing gently. Suddenly, the engine stopped.

I looked up worriedly. The pilot was obviously going to land in the field beside me. A few innocently grazing sheep were about to get a nasty surprise. He was close to the ground now and then he was down. The wheels rumbled noisily along the rough grass. Would he stop before the hedge or would I have to bravely pull him from the mangled wreckage?

Happily, he stopped in time. As I approached, he climbed out, smiled boyishly and said, “That was fun.”

~

Sheila Gray’s Biography

See story 142.

150: FRIENDLY SMILE

by Sandra Orellana

He wanted a kindly gesture from the lively party. Usually he sat quietly, but this time he behaved as normally as he could to be noticed. People didn't.

Quickly, he entered the restroom and sadly saw himself in the mirror, asking himself, "Is it my ugly face or my awful taste in clothes?"

He walked out bravely, towards the people, but they hardly noticed him again. He asked God, "Why do you make me feel so terribly bad? They think I'm not lavishly important, with no title or money." He finished dejectedly, saying, "Yes, people can make you feel uncomfortably inhuman."

~

Sandra Orellana's Biography

Sandra Orellana was born in El Paso, Texas on the border of México. Her passions are tennis and her students. She reaches out to the Chichimecas and the homeless. She spends her time living in México city and San Miguel Allende.

151: OFF THE WAGON

by Glen Donaldson

It had been kookily named 'Pistachio Cusperson's lifelong wish to personally witness a proton aurora in the night sky'. Now, with that moment properly upon him, he was foolishly, inauspiciously and, some might say, downright pathetically passed out on the backseat of his car with only his loyal frenemy Jack Daniels next to him for company.

It was a soberingly considered thought for the unemployed bartender that the next time the electrically-charged, magnificently-coloured and rarely-glimpsed sun-particles light show came to town, he'd need to be off the wagon rather than numbingly blacked out in the back of one.

~

Glen Donaldson's Biography

Glen Donaldson knows it takes two mystery writers to fit a lightbulb – one to screw the bulb almost all the way in and the other to give a surprising twist at the end.

www.goosefleshsite.wordpress.com

152: NAVIGATIONALLY MISPLACED

by Merryn Byrne

The young man unhelpfully gestured instructionally to the map with irrevocably irritating smugness. His painstakingly maintained fingernails infuriatingly tapped the smudgily, badly printed, undesirably illegible surface. Upon further maddeningly useless, unintelligible yet artfully executed gesticulation, we abandoned our poorly constructed attempt to communicate for help.

Uselessly and directionlessly wandering, hopefully searching for our seemingly impossibly and unappealingly misplaced destination was our only sanely viable option. So, unwillingly, we tiredly and frustratedly undertook it. Eventually defeated, we grumpily found an alternative, cheaply dirty hotel to temporarily house us as we depressedly admitted we were hopelessly lost and absurdly monolingual.

~

Merryn Byrne's Biography

No author biography supplied.

153: THE MACBETHS TAKE DELIVERY OF A FLAT-PACK BED

by Margaret Edwards

Lady Macbeth (uneasily): Read the instructions carefully this time.

Macbeth (insouciantly): So how desperately difficult can it be? (Nonchalantly discards the instruction sheets.) Four strong planks, 26 wooden slats... it seemeth All Birnam Wood is bubble-wrapped in here. And Duncan imminent, expecting a bedroom ready. Ha. Only 18 dowels and, crucially, no Allen key enclosed safe in the box – I said: NO ALLEN KEY.

Lady Macbeth (exasperatedly): Here it lies plainly under the instructions.

Macbeth (incredulously): Oh. (Curses.) But it fitteth uselessly. AARRGGHH... Woman, why bring you that knife?

Lady Macbeth (dangerously low): Just do it. Now. (Blade glitters merrily.)

~

Margaret Edwards' Biography

See story 146.

154: LOVE –VS– MONEY

by Glen Donaldson

"Unlike your naively-intentioned good self, I'm in this for the money, not the applause," caustically retorted Jim, the avalanche insurance salesman to his regrettably, lawfully-acknowledged half-brother Cedric the circus clown on the occasion of Cedric annoyingly presuming to give him inappropriately and inopportunely unsolicited career advice.

"Applause is a receipt, not a bill," replied Cedric enigmatically, honking his oversized red nose cartoonishly for effect, yet unable to disguise the traces of anger and indignation hissing revealingly from him like a hot air balloon.

"While you may measure success in money," Cedric added quotationally, "I measure it in non-receipted, unaudited love."

~

Glen Donaldson's Biography

See story 151.

155: LEE AND FRIENDS

by Zaheer Babar

The mothership loomed largely above the small hero spaceship, firing deadly missiles randomly. Manoeuvring spritely in-between the oncoming death-traps, the heroic spaceship fired a thin, bright laser beam, hitting the mothership in her vulnerable middle. The mothership exploded violently.

Lee top-scored on the arcade 'Space Outvaders'.

"Yes," he shouted loudly.

"Yeah," chorused his friends triumphantly, fists pumping the air ecstatically.

In the bar the crowds were chatting noisily. The group of friends sat down at a nearby table. Pints were spilled carelessly and crisps stuffed in mouths greedily. The night ended quietly as the group headed home.

Happy-Lee the end.

~

Zaheer Babar's Biography

Zaheer Babar was born in Pakistan and moved to the UK when he was less than two years old. Bred and living in Worcester, England, he is married with four children.

156: BUTTING OUT

by Glen Donaldson

Hapless Jim Burgundy had neglectfully failed to notice the additional ‘t’ in the spelling of the word ‘buttler’ when he unwittingly replied to a job ad for a live in male servant.

Regrettably, only later was he to discover that his uniform necessitated the wearing of a hospital-gown-like ‘open-back’ onesie that not only unequivocally put the ‘butt’ into buttler but also somewhat absurdly provided a literal interpretation of the age old adage ‘nothing good happens in the basement’.

Tropeingly, the buttler did do it, but only up until the first pay-cycle fortnight, whereupon he tactically tended his resignation.

~

Glen Donaldson’s Biography

See story 151.

157: HILLARY AND DONALD

by Stephanie Sybliss

Hillary and Donald smiled, while viciously and sweetly he played gamely on his trumpet, luring all to follow, jovially.

"Dear Hillary, show us your lightly jolly speech."

"Not likely," she apprehensively spoke carefully. "I see how bullishly you have forced the world to see how brutishly you can sickly glide."

"How dare you speak so wrongly of my wily wiles and my charmingly, handsomely, devilish dealings with people?"

"Dear Donald, you're competently, brilliantly clever," Hillary said happily.

Hillary crossed her fingers secretly and left the podium unfortunately.

Funnily ironic, how trumpery is often appealingly bright but usually not for long.

~

Stephanie Sybliss's Biography

There's a big clue as to what I've been watching in the media by the stories that spill out of my brain. Sad or what, eh? You can catch my kooky nonsense on my blog too.

www.wordpress76354.wordpress.com

158: MARRIAGE IN THE CROSS HAIRS

by June Lee

"Anything for my hubby wubby teddy bear," rapturously enthused newly married Rachel Cornrows, not fully realising the intolerably demanding extent of the hair-cutting duties she had just agreed to for her husband, who unbeknownstedly to her was a direct descendent – genealogically speaking – of the Blackwoods Werewolf clan and therefore regrettably carried the active XY chromosome that predisposed him to hirsuteness.

Fatefully, their week-long honeymoon on Lake Strand freak-of-naturedly included four consecutively spaced full moon nights. For innocently intentioned Rachel, marriage would indeed spell 'transformation' and seriously bad hair days would feature all too prominently.

~

June Lee's Biography

June Lee's work has appeared in *Pure Sludge, The Don't Bother Review, Dross Monthly, Garbage Hole, Dreadful Fiction, Regrettable Reads, Take Pity Magazine, The Poor Press, D Class Scribes, Leftover Quarterly* and *Useless Words.*

She is forthcoming in *Give It A Miss.*

June Lee is known for her consistent use of the unreliable narrator.

159: STRICTLY EDWARD'S DANCING

by Stephanie Sybliss

Edward strode proudly, masterfully onto the perfectly, sparkly dance floor. He began to shake and shimmy. With his hands he purposefully made shapes that constantly transformed him into a mincing, tremendously broadly-bellied bean of a man.

His costume glittered brilliantly, with buttons gaping dangerously while scarily they pointed directly at the cameras. His partner smiled enthusiastically, the audience giggled insanely, joyfully waiting for the madness to be over. Edward lifted her swiftly and she nearly fell at a height so terrifyingly hazardous.

The ballsy Balls eagerly awaits the verdict, hoping he will be able to shine next week again.

~

Stephanie Sybliss's Biography

See story 157.

160: WRITING BY ROTE

by Kathryn Watson

Click.

Tentatively, she selected words and arranged them on the page. Scanning from abnormally to zestily. Mustn't forget her favourites. The seductive onomatopoeism of cheerfully, blissfully, daintily and owlishly. And the luscious silkiness of smoothly.

Her mind wandered. Words swam joyfully before her eyes. A stirring breeze drifted through the open window. Dozily she lifted her chin from her hand. But where to start?

To list is not enough – the words need a home, a story. No, she couldn't do it. This wasn't a good idea. After all, what is an adverb?

~

Kathryn Watson's Biography

Kathryn Watson, although not a Time Traveler's Wife, enjoys the sedate excitements of domesticity which her home in south west France affords in spades. Running a gite, chasing puppies, cooking for husband and friends, writing when possible, makes up the rest of her life.

161: CAUSTIC SODA

by Kathryn Watson

As she caught the eye of the customer, a chill ran down her spine. Bitter memories flooded back and cruel images swam before her. This was her chance.

He drank greedily as he talked boastfully. Lazily taking in his surroundings he mockingly glanced in her direction. So much time and so many changes; had he recognised her? He left without a backward look, his step faltering.

Victoriously, she swiftly slid the glass from the bar and washed it zealously. She smiled inwardly. Rightly or wrongly, finally she had triumphed.

~

Kathryn Watson's Biography

See story 160.

162: LADY IN WAITING

by Kathryn Watson

Stealthily she moved forward, the morning dew soaking deliciously between her toes. Usually, she was the last one out, but this morning she had eagerly awaited the click of the lock. Quietly and carefully, she crossed the lawn, barely leaving a trace. Sleepily, she settled into her special spot. Lazily, she slowly stretched and yawned. Her heart pitter-pattered in her chest.

Soon, she knew it would be soon.

Suddenly, she heard the sound she had been anticipating. She sprang forward gleefully. Her earnest wait was rewarded – the butcher's van always came early on a Tuesday.

~

Kathryn Watson's Biography

See story 160.

163: POLICE LINE: DO NOT CROSS

by Verity Hemp

"Well, well, well," he barked loudly, as always, inserting himself forcefully into the situation.

D.I. Parker squinted curiously, crouched knee-crackingly and suddenly hissed excitedly, "Come quickly."

Disappointingly, she wanted (and rightly so) to look carefully at the body.

He thought inwardly and secretly of how in television dramas, female partners flirted brazenly, kissed passionately and often followed obediently. D.I. Parker conversely talked cleverly, worked unceasingly and drank heavily, but never acted seductively.

She continued heatedly, "The man fell heavily."

He pulled on his gloves reluctantly. Another night spent sleeplessly.

~

Verity Hemp's Biography

No author biography supplied.

164: LITTLE LAZARUS CAT

by J. Rosina Harlow

Yellow eyes stared listlessly, unblinkingly. We rushed him in, sorrowfully, cradled carefully in a towel.

Painkillers were administered intravenously, blood tests taken tenderly.

In the brightly lit consultation room the vet quoted the emergency fee almost imperceptibly gleefully (so now all of us are poorly).

As the rain came down lashingly, we headed back home sombrely and, wakefully, lovingly, we watched.

18 years reached miraculously, we both agreed, tearfully.

Morning came rapidly and we awoke nervously to hear a cat scratching delightedly, destructively (and really quite cheerfully).

He sneaked up on us snoopily, playfully.

Our little Lazarus cat.

~

J. Rosina Harlow's Biography

See story 107.

165: OVER-CONFIDENT WOMAN

by Namita Mukherjee

You are always trying to dominate everyone confidently, pretending to be very happily married, but you are not.

Now you lie regretfully that you had thought foolishly that you are cleverer than everybody, but you are not. You fearfully denied that you are isolated, unpopular and neglected. You're trying to ruin other people's peace of mind cleverly but you fail – unsuccessfully. You put other people down gladly. You want recognition for your work greatly. You insult yourself unconsciously when you praise yourself proudly. Your mind always thinks about yourself joyfully, you do not look at yourself when you criticize others jealously.

~

Namita Mukherjee's Biography

No author biography supplied.

166: ADVICE FOR PASSENGERS

by Florence Caplin

Intentionally avoiding eye contact, Sam surreptitiously curls her fingers around a slightly damp newspaper. Her vision dashes deftly from the tram window to the boldly printed 'Chilli Likely Causes Cancer Experts Say'. Anywhere but the other passenger.

After fidgeting uncomfortably for a while, she glances uneasily up at the Greek man across from her. He quietly sips from a water bottle. As the maddeningly noiseless compartment rolls on, Sam considers something carefully.

Smiling triumphantly, her eyes meet the stranger's. He smiles back. Politely. Swallowing a tankful of air, she speaks deliberately, "You might want to cut down on Thai food."

~

Florence Caplin's Biography

No author biography supplied.

167: BRANDY LEE

by Joseph Hancock

Brandy Lee boldly assuredly, yet delicately, compassionately keeps the peace in the outrageously, occasionally shamelessly, eerily spasmodically diverse city of Los Angelesly. She successfully righteously stylishly applies the law ethically and intelligently. While helpfully amazingly remaining agreeably, always consistently kindly non judgmentally, justly delivers the law to the unruly.

Brandy Lee occasionally stealthily, especially after a stressfully tremendously vigorously challenging day, indulges in violently wickedly recklessly ferociously sounds of unabashedly loudly played heavy metal. And what I knowingly ask mysteriously adorns noisily supremely systematically brutal sounds better for Brandy Lee other than sushi, splendidly appropriately covered in? Joyously lovingly intensely jubilantly consumed wasabi.

~

Joseph Hancock's Biography

Joe Hancock lives in Greenwich, Southern New Jersey, with his dog, Bug. A musician by trade, he is new to the writing field and loving every minute of it.

www.facebook.com/joseph.hancock.9480

168: PROCRASTINATION CAN STUNT YOUR GROWTH

by Lesley Truchet

I'm blatantly procrastinating again. Instead, I could visit my mother in law, reluctantly. Read a novel, indulgently. Pay some bills, grudgingly. Take a bath, crucially. Weed the garden, laboriously. Clean the car, aridly. Go for a walk, breathlessly. Watch television, detachedly. Tackle the washing up, apathetically. Cut my pudgy toe nails, problematically. Re-decorate my kitchen, abhorrently. Defrost the freezer, tediously. Make some coffee, enthusiastically. Take a nap, willingly. Do some laundry, essentially. Perform some housework, dismally.

I settle down instead to write this adverbially abounding autography. Today I will grow a little.

~

Lesley Truchet's Biography

See story 125.

169: JUST MAKING IT TO THE SHOWER

by Bryan Smith

He stood wearily and impatiently as, sluggishly, she dragged herself slowly out of bed and reluctantly and falteringly made her way to the shower. Having drunk excessively the night before, she was incredibly hung over.

Unenthusiastically, and somewhat miraculously, she completed the journey. Suddenly, she stumbled and fell heavily. Uncontrollably, she sobbed out the pain experienced.

“I need help,” she cried pathetically. “This is excruciatingly painful.”

He laughed relentlessly as, unsympathetically, he eventually helped her out of the shower. “Just desserts for a frequently practicing alcoholic,” he declared scathingly.

Staring venomously, she said, “I love you passionately too.”

~

Bryan Smith’s Biography

Am relatively new to fiction writing – short stories/short plays. Several have been published/performed.

Substantial number of non-fiction publications from a career in management consultancy-books, articles, book reviews. Also, many years as editor of an international journal.

170: HIS FAVOURITE MONSTER

by Mark Johnson

He voraciously watched them all: the enormously powerful King Ghidorah, the eternally victorious Godzilla, the tremendously worthless Gigan.

Through them all, he ultimately chose Mothra as his favourite. Violently attacking with hurricane-force winds, flying easily over and away from his enemies, Mothra zestily seized his imagination.

Unfortunately, something of a pervert, he oddly imagined himself six inches tall, lustfully spending his time knavishly attempting to seduce Mothra's twin fairies as they lovingly sang the Song of Mothra.

Churlishly imagined.

~

Mark Johnson's Biography

Mark Johnson is a writer living in Mississippi. He has a wife, two sons and two cats.

www.markjohnsonauthor.com

171: NEW ABODE

by Betty Hattersley

Normally eccentric, her gardening idealistic was ordinary on an everyday basis.

She spent numerous hours on her project.

Endeavouring, I politely asked some informative questions (obviously without sounding too inquisitive of course).

Astounded as dusk was falling, I immediately visualised a magical, delicate illumination appearing from a tree stump in the centre of her elegant garden.

"Why are those colourful, reflecting, flickering illuminations glowing from your garden?"

Casually, she informed me that fairies had taken residence in the tree stump and were having a party to celebrate their new abode.

What more could one say?

~

Betty Hattersley's Biography

I've been writing for many years and have had numerous poems and short stories published in anthologies, newspapers, calendars and magazines.

I've written a small book (yet to be published) about the funny side of my outside catering days.

172: HAPPILY EVER AFTER

by Lorna Gillies

Breathtakingly beautiful in her gloriously decadent couture gown, face gently covered by a delicately laced veil, she elegantly and gracefully glided down the aisle. Her dazzlingly silky hair was swept up in a carefully created array of curls, creatively festooned with deliciously vibrant coloured crystals. Her devilishly handsome, ridiculously wealthy and incredibly, undeniably faithful groom lovingly gazed at her as she moved gently towards him.

It was all so sickeningly perfect and with every bone in my body I secretly despised them both and all they stood for.

Graciously, however, I opened my bible and brought the congregation to attention.

~

Lorna Gillies' Biography

I'm from the Isle of Skye but currently live and teach in Adelaide. I'm obsessed with two things – Cavalier King Charles Spaniels and storytelling. I'm clumsy, slightly deranged and mildly alarmed about sharing my scribblings with the world.

173: SITUATION VACANT

by Paul Phillips

Currently rapidly expanding, our client is actively seeking to permanently appoint a dynamically, demonstrably effective individual to smoothly and harmoniously manage change immediately and, eventually, going forward.

Probably already working impactfully in a closely related or similarly associated sector, you are quantifiably capable of thinking deep, acting fast and seriously making a difference. Additionally, you should be highly able to communicate extremely clearly, confidently and professionally – verbally, orally and literally.

Finally, however, we are no longer entirely able to promise that you will be generously rewarded for your commitment, only that remuneration will typically be received, sometimes.

Apply yesterday.

~

Paul Phillips' Biography

Paul Phillips writes short and long fiction across a variety of genres. He lives in Derbyshire with several humans and a hairy brown thing.

www.bypaulphillips.com

174: DEFTLY MOVES THE NIGHT

by Ellena Restrick

Softly softly catchy monkey. She knew she just had to be patient as she moved slowly towards the target.

Gently. Not long now. Quickly in and out. The blade shone splendidly in the pale moonlight, glimmering like a slowly dying star. She stared contemplatively at the sky; seldom were there such utterly beautiful nights in London town. It pained her to have to perform such a heinous act against this canvas; she would paint the stars with the blood of the dead.

She suddenly felt cold metal against the back of her head. Quickly she turned.

"I'd stop right now if I were you."

~

Ellena Restrick's Biography

No author biography supplied.

175: TELE-VISUALLY UNAPPEALING

by Helen P Stephens

The quietly dormant TV in the corner suddenly burst into life, garishly bright with a thunderously deafening soundtrack.

Two overly smiley celebrities walked purposefully onto a stage. Their widely grinning faces were soaking up the unnecessarily persistent applause from an audience that was obediently following their cues from a group of absurdly eager runners, enthusiastically wielding oversized cards with instructions for appropriately reacting to everything that happened on stage – like they couldn't realistically be trusted to appropriately emote.

Len's brow furrowed deeply as he instinctively recoiled in horror and quickly picked up the remote control and deliberately pressed the off button.

~

Helen P Stephens' Biography

Helen P Stephens spends much of her time writing, whether it's press releases, blog posts or funding applications. Her debut novel, *Inspired By Night*, was published in 2014 (under the pen name L.E. May) by Xcite Books.

www.helenpstephens.co.uk

176: WALKIES

by Daniel Prestwich

At last, the master's delightfully dulcet voice sang through the early morning's crisply cold air. "Mutley, walkies."

Mutley energetically and enthusiastically ran past his despairingly patient master in a bid to get outside. Embarrassingly, he trudged back, waiting, tremblingly agitated. The lead clicked satisfyingly onto the collar.

At last, they were outside. The overwhelmingly, invitingly teasing smells came from every direction. Left or right? Right. How satisfyingly, predictably prosaic. Fabulously empty fields stretched before them.

At last, the lead was worryingly removed and Mutley joyfully bounded off to explore the timidly waiting world.

He would grudgingly return, at last.

~

Daniel Prestwich's Biography

Daniel is an English language teacher, currently residing in Spain. He enjoys his peripatetic lifestyle as it gives him the chance to witness and hear many fascinating stories which are a great source of inspiration.

www.dansscribblings.wordpress.com

177: A CRY FOR HELP

by Michael Rumsey

Painstakingly, I completed the lengthy intricately designed Census Form. Jokingly, under ‘Children In The Home’, I wrote ‘two – soon to be three’. I sat back with mighty relief.

Unexpectedly, my satisfied calm was suddenly and thoroughly shattered. My normally serene, highly-pregnant wife gushed piercingly from the bathroom, “Water’s broke. Call emergency.”

Madly and frantically, I made a dash for the phone. Actively Alert Ambulances would hastily respond.

“Quickly,” she continued imploringly, “phone Pete’s Permanently Prompt Plumbers. Our wickedly woefully installed centrally heated radiator has annoyingly and menacingly sprung an alarmingly large leak.”

~

Michael Rumsey’s Biography

See story 104.

178: MR AKABAKA

by Mumtaz Waliat

Standing in front of the sink and mirror readily, Mr Akabaka washed his face energetically, brushed his teeth rigidly and combed his hair imperatively.

Finished, he went hurriedly into the living room where his wife was waiting impatiently.

"Who's going to shave that beard? Your dad?" she said arguably.

He went back into the bathroom obediently.

He winced melodramatically as shaving began. It was over before he knew it and he rubbed his hand over his smooth skin contently.

His wife looked at him attentively. "Who did you shave for?"

"Well, there's this young lady at work," Mr Akabaka retorted swiftly.

~

Mumtaz Waliat's Biography

Mumtaz is Mr Akabaka, or is according to his wife. He is happily married to Saima with four children. This is his first foray in writing short stories where it has actually been published and he thoroughly enjoyed it.

179: NO

by Sarah Aston

“Emphatically, unequivocally, categorically my answer is no,” I blithely told him. He reacted sanguinely, calmly, proudly, yet with a hint of frailty visibly evident.

I remained resolutely independent, yet mostly polite, at least in company where this was socially necessary.

He asked again, more nervously yet earnestly. Naturally I did not reply affirmatively.

He went away, periodically. Surprisingly, unexpectedly I found I missed him, albeit occasionally.

Irritatingly, time passed more slowly when he was absent. I passed my days interminably in fittingly womanly distractions.

Eventually, quite remarkably, he asked again. Immediately my heart leapt.

Reader, I married him.

At Pemberley.

~

Sarah Aston’s Biography

Sarah lives in rural Wiltshire. After a long career in management, she wants to get back to using her imagination. Sarah’s always written songs but this is her first attempt at a story. For that she thanks/blames Mark.

180: HEAVEN IN A GLASS

by Jamie Caddick

The pint of real ale sat dutifully on the bar. There it rested beautifully, and there I watched it expectantly.

The glass was refreshingly cool, almost sensuously so. Occasionally, a drip would cheekily trickle down the glass as if to tease me in an erotically-charged exchange of blissfully enticing promise.

I seriously considered a packet of pork scratchings. Nope, I reproached myself scornfully. Indubitably, that won't do. To obscenely ingest those marvellously indulgent and hedonistically sublime crunchy pig rinds would be sacrilege.

I scolded myself censoriously – then enthusiastically wolfed back a liquid mouthful in all its lubriciously, gratifyingly pleasurable glory.

~

Jamie Caddick's Biography

Voltaire, Bukowski, Hemingway, Caddick. They've all been named in the same sentence. Well, that's what Jamie likes to tell himself in his never-ending quest for grandiose, literary glory. He resides in Bristol with an insatiable penchant for good books, fine women, quirky films and real ale (sometimes all at the same time).

181: IN THE CORNER OFFICE

by Kate Vane

Silkily whispering into the phone, she's opaquely distant in the darkly cool light at the achingly vast matte desk. He listens closely, crisply silhouetted by the cleanly sealed plate glass, glancing unseeingly at the indifferently continuing city.

"It's done," she says emphatically. She wipes the phone and the desk fluidly, erasing her fingerprints irrevocably.

He pads imperceptibly across the opulently austere flooring. They close the door softly, after she mists the air briskly to delete the scent of their memory.

"They are sending premium paper towels urgently." They take their brushes and their buckets determinedly and continue their work, stoically.

~

Kate Vane's Biography

Kate Vane lives in Devon. She writes crime and literary fiction and is the author of two novels, *Recognition* and *Not the End*. Her third novel, *The Former Chief Executive*, will be published in 2017.

www.katevane.wordpress.com

182: THE ENTRY

by Lilian Indombera Musundi

The crickets sung sweetly, melodically lulling the night creatures to sleep. The night leisurely set in; the dogs barking gladly and gratifyingly, played ready for the night watch. She ardently patrolled the homestead intensely reciting the Rosary, making sure the back and side gate were closed and the front left open. Morning gradually but avidly kissed the day goodbye.

The dogs barked fiercely, announcing his wee hour's arrival. Staggering, soothingly puffing an embassy.

"Baby, baby," he called hesitantly. When there was no reply, he bellowed, "BABY," loudly, firmly and unfalteringly.

She jumped promptly, abruptly from the bed, as if it contained safari ants.

~

Lilian Indombera Musundi's Biography

Lilian Indombera Musundi is a Kenyan writer, poet, master story teller and performer with a passion for life and expressing it in words. She has published two children's storybooks with Pauline's Publications: *Sheila and Other Stories* and *The Mango Sellers*.

183: FALLING FLYINGLY

by Jenny Gaitskell

The day after his breathtakingly narrow escape, Trevor received an ostensibly official letter. It was painfully verbose and initially baffling, but he eventually understood that a hitherto obscure secret service branch confidently expected that he would freely, voluntarily and unquestioningly abstain from any further attempts to fly, or immediately and summarily receive something obliquely described as trimming.

Trevor's earlier experience had felt distinctly and terrifyingly like falling uncontrollably, but the letter inevitably made him irresistibly curious. He began modestly, jumping from chairs, adding height progressively until finally climbing his roof, only to discover a darkly uniformed visitor waving shears menacingly.

~

Jenny Gaitskell's Biography

Mostly writing. Likes making up words and crossing genres. Blogs weekly on writing with a smile on her face.

Find Jenny on Twitter: @JennyGaitskell

184: PIRATE TREASURE

by Sarah Wilde

He roared fearsomely, the bitter wind tearing at his straggly blond hair. Raw emotion tingled down his knobbly spine.

"It's mine," he screeched victoriously.

Unexpectedly, he lost his tentative grasp on the very slippery box. Turning gracefully in the air it paused hesitantly, then slowly dropped towards the roaring sea. Frantically scrabbling on the seaweed covered rocks, the tantalisingly close, decadently glittering treasure chest slipped lazily past his fingers. The translucently, tumultuous waters crashed loudly into the base of the towering rocky cliffs. The boiling, shivering crests of the coruscating waves closed quickly over the opulent box. Gone now forever.

~

Sarah Wilde's Biography

Sarah spends as much time as possible adventuring with her young family and a puppy. She lives on a river in sunny Devon and has a blog about living on a boat, writing and taking photos.

www.sarahontarquilla.blogspot.com

185: FACEBOOK

by Sarah Wilde

Stunningly beautiful photos of a romantically perfect wedding. The hauntingly cryptic cry for attention. The pleadingly urgent status of someone desperately seeking help; for homework, plumbers or to find someone mysteriously missing. Gaudy photos of a fantastically amazing party, the status that alarmingly spreads ridiculously fake news. Madly ranting pessimists and randomly destructive trolls. Achingly familiar faces appearing in photos taken long ago or far away. Appallingly poor jokes, amusingly wry memes. The startlingly happy stories, the victoriously announced good news. The genuinely touching support, the intuitively offered help. The virtually real friendships. Addictively, slippery, lovingly, Facebook.

~

Sarah Wilde's Biography

See story 184.

186: BY THE BABBLING BROOK

by Mathijs Koenraadt

Mother goose lay quietly in the softly blowing wind by the calmly babbling brook, intimately sleeping beside her chicks. Then, a ferociously wild dog inconspicuously and unsuspectingly approached them.

A vigilantly awoken father goose assertively sounded the alarm by quacking incessantly. Showmanly flapping his wings, he cleverly but dangerously distracted the dog, deceivingly luring it to him.

Woken abruptly, mother goose instantly commandeered her hesitantly complying chicks into the water.

Seeing his family escape the dog easily, father goose immediately dropped his act, swiftly took off and later rejoined his family safely.

~

Mathijs Koenraadt's Biography

Mathijs Koenraadt is a writer and philosopher from the Netherlands.

www.koenraadt.info

187: SPACE CATERPILLAR

by Nick Davis

Skilfully and audaciously he quickly, but anxiously, removed his helmet and loudly shooed out the beautifully green and fairly fat space caterpillar rarely seen around these parts. Promptly, yet cautiously, he placed the helmet back on.

"I don't know what you were laughing at, they'd eat through your wires if they got inside," quipped the Spaceman, straightforwardly.

Roma, a stylishly yet suspiciously super-smart robot, continued to laugh. Then, intently, "Amazingly, they're genetically obedient. And almost always only eat each other."

"I'll consider keeping one as a pet next time." Instantly and intentionally the spaceman enthusiastically jumped on the caterpillar. Fatally.

~

Nick Davis's Biography

Find Nick on Twitter: @nickofthesea

188: POSSIBLY, MAYBE, ALWAYS

by Melanie Rees

Ley skilfully jumped onto the sofa. She innocently picked up her walking lead and glanced at Mack ever so sheepishly.

Walkies. She barked optimistically.

"Possibly." Mack always mysteriously understood Ley.

Ley repeatedly padded in circles on the cushion and determinedly pawed her lead.

Walkies. She proudly barked.

"Maybe, Ley. Let me quickly do a few things first and we'll definitely go for walks."

Walkies. She deliberately dropped her lead directly in Mack's lap and forcibly nudged Mack's hand away from his computer. *WALKIES*. She barked piercingly.

"Always," Mack dramatically grumbled. He deftly clipped on Ley's lead. "You always get your way."

~

Melanie Rees's Biography

Melanie Rees is an Australian author. Her fiction and poetry have happily and magically appeared in markets such as *Apex, The School Magazine, Aurealis* and *Daily Science Fiction*. Inquisitively, you can learn more on her website.

www.flexirees.wordpress.com

189: TEARS ON THE MOUNTAIN

by Teddy Hester

Cat rarely cried. It was just often so tremendously girly. But after an accidentally and embarrassingly hard fall on a really ridiculously easy bunny slope (while incidentally snapping the tip off her delightfully, fashionably pink ski), tears flowed mightily.

She swiped at them frantically fast, miserably aware of quite an appallingly lot of bitingly cold wind freezing her smoothly and effusively spilt drops into some very rigidly-laced lattices on her quite rosily reddened cheeks.

In order to stand sturdily enough outside to get her shiveringly chilled body inside, the infuriatingly silly bawling really, truly needed to stop. Immediately.

~

Teddy Hester's Biography

Teddy Hester is a retired elementary teacher now writing novels. She enjoys skiing bunny slopes, cooking pepperoni lasagna and playing hide-n-seek or fetch with her kitty, Geranium.

www.teddyhester.com

190: BEACHSIDE DISTRACTIONS

by Helmine Kemp

Jauntily walking along the crowded esplanade, I joyfully revel in the invigorating breeze. I nimbly sidestep the people robotically transfixed on their phones. They hungrily devour the trivia bursting vividly on their screens. Their eyes blindly focused so they don't see the sparkling waves noisily splashing onto the sandy beach. Their ears are so voluntarily and completely deafened that they don't hear the joyful screeches of playful children, or even the raucous squabbling of seagulls hungrily and opportunistically scavenging stray oddments of fallen food. Their hands swiftly and jerkily scroll through screens, narrowly missing the off-switch that could instantly deliver them a beautiful life.

~

Helmine Kemp's Biography

Helmine Kemp, an aspiring novelist based in Adelaide, Australia, has written a, as yet unpublished, literary thriller, *Deadly Secrets*. Her first published short story appears in *Fledglings: an Anthology* and she's delighted to be included in *Adverbially Challenged Volume 2*.

191: LILY AND THE COOKIE JAR

by Adriane Kirkbright

Gingerly, Lily tiptoed in the kitchen, eyes curiously analysing the ceramic cookie jar unbelievably high on the counter. Incredibly small three-year olds could hardly reach the counter, even on their preciously tiny tippy-toes.

But sugary chocolate chip cookies waited.

Delightfully encouraged, Lily bravely climbed, greeted by her satisfyingly tasty new crumbly friends.

"Yummy," said Lily excitedly. In all her enthusiasm, she accidentally smeared chocolate on her tremendously fancy dress.

Mummy came in, laughing joyfully at her cookie-crumbled little one innocently enjoying her sweet treat.

"I am full in my really little belly," Lily said, innocently patting her adorably chocolated tummy.

~

Adriane Kirkbright's Biography

No author biography supplied.

192: THE CONVENT

by Lydia Stott

Quietly, the nun slyly crept across the room, surreptitiously. Despite her suspiciously nonchalant facial expression, the Holy father forgivingly forgave her. Shockingly, the nun continued backwards and forwards in a blatantly eye-drawing and unmistakeably evident way and drew some glaringly pointed looks from her sisters.

Eventually, the nun silently left the room, followed frustratedly by the eyes of some grumpily hangry Christians. Peculiarly, she appeared brightly behind a pillar, with a teenage boy.

He sneakily handed over something brilliantly shining that had obviously been polished frequently. The cross from behind the father who always preached boringly.

Oh God.

~

Lydia Stott's Biography

Lydia Stott is a 14-year-old who has always had a passion for story-telling. Although she wishes to study maths further, she believes writing will always be a part of her life and she one day hopes be a published novelist.

193: SNOO GLEE

by Rebecca Henderson

The curiously-coloured cat bounded quietly across the decidedly dismal landscape.

Deeply concerned with the very lively creature she quickly discovered not two leaps into the dreary surroundings, the cat dutifully sniffed the incredibly intriguing form before her. Her nose twinged painfully. Shudderingly ugly, the garishly-formed body hardly seemed to fit satisfactorily in reality.

Effortlessly abandoning the scene, the cat eerily snuck away, eyes alight.

The especially ugly creature sighed sadly. Eventually someone would come along, enthusiastically anxious to meet a new friend. The creature gazed expectantly in the direction of the fleeing cat.

Two bright eyes gaped endearingly. Expectantly. Wistfully.

~

Rebecca Henderson's Biography

See story 116.

194: PRINTING THE LAST PAGE OF JANE EYRE

by Margaret Edwards

Today, dreamed Mr Longbody, he'd finally be inked and used.

The printer sorted letters briskly. Eagerly, they squeezed into the composing stick *Reader, I married him* and Mr Longbody became wildly excited. The printer hesitated, then seized Mr Longbody determinedly, slamming him in at the end.

Blackly, squidgily, the ink coated his virginal silver body. Wonderful.

The printer stopped, appalled.

"I can't do this," he gasped, "however coaxingly Miss Bronte pleads."

Mr Longbody was ejected unceremoniously, but still smiling stickily, suddenly foreseeing his glorious zenith in the era of emails and excitable texts.

~

Margaret Edwards' Biography

See story 146.

195: THE PRINCESS AND THE BUTTERFLY

by Sophie Mulvaney

Once there was a girl called Rose. She was constantly bored – so bored that if she didn't do something about it she would blow up. BOOM.

One day, Rose's mummy made her play outside. Outside there was a scary bear. A beautiful butterfly glided past. Then Rose shouted, "HELP, SAVE ME."

The butterfly came and saved her, then picked her a flower and whispered into her ear, "You're magical, Princess Rose."

Rose said, "WHAT? MAGICAL? PRINCESS?" She noticed that she was alone inside. Rose was never bored again. She wrote a story about this and you're reading it right NOW.

~

Sophie Mulvaney's Biography

I'm six years old and my favourite colour is rainbow, and my favorite flower is a rose. I like to watch *My Little Pony*, especially Rainbow Dash, and in *The Trolls* I like Poppy the best.

196: HARRY POTTER – WHAT REALLY HAPPENED

by Emma Mulvaney

Harry Potter's story, as you know, is about Voldemort trying to kill Harry. But what really happened is nothing like that.

Voldemort entered the house just after Lily and James came back from their honeymoon. Lily screamed at the top of her voice, then James came running down and started casting spells at Voldemort, so Voldemort had to fight back.

Eventually, Lily and James died, but then Voldemort looked into Harry's green eyes. He quickly took Harry away, trying to dodge the people trying to kill him. One hit Harry on the head – that's how he got his scar.

Voldemort quickly disappeared and never returned until 10 years later...

~

Emma Mulvaney's Biography

I'm nine years old and live with my mum and dad and two sisters. My hobbies are playing with my BFF, swimming, playing guitar and reading *Harry Potter*. I hope you enjoy my story. Happy Reading.

197: THE FURIOUSLY FURIOUS SNOWSTORM

by Kate Mulvaney

The wind was furiously charging towards me as I whooshed by at at-least 50mph. I think I was definitely winning. For one thing, I hadn't fallen off yet.

The wind started to strengthen and I knew I had to resign, so I turned around and started galloping back home. The weather witch must of hated me this morning because my worst fear came true – snow. Well, it isn't exactly my worst fear. More like Biscuit's – my chestnut horse.

"Whoa, girl," I yelled as the horse started getting completely out of control. "Whoa, girl."

She suddenly stopped and I flew forward. Luckily, I managed to hold on.

Biscuit wouldn't budge. I had to get off and drag her back home which, believe me, you wouldn't want to do in the middle of a furiously furious snowstorm.

~

Kate Mulvaney's Biography

I'm Kate Mulvaney, I'm in year 7. My hobbies are horse riding, keyboard, Guides, writing, cooking, hanging out with friends and being a big sister. I love animals (including snake/spiders), *Harry Potter* (I'm number one fan) and thriller rides like rollercoasters.

198: REGRETTABLY

by Binyamin Bashir

She cheered on merrily as the singer sang devotedly. She looked on wonderingly and vivaciously as fireworks fired victoriously.

The audience roared powerfully and fell about foolishly, madly, obediently. They swung their bodies mindlessly and knocked about others selfishly.

She gasped sharply as she was pushed and pulled occasionally. Eventually, she cheered rarely and no longer spoke happily. She felt excessively sickly and looked about sternly.

Her temperature rose rapidly as she fell back, fainting regrettably.

~

Binyamin Bashir's Biography

Binyamin is a 20 year old law student living in Cambridge. With a creative imagination and a flair for writing, he hopes to have a fantasy novel published in the foreseeable future (or at the very least – completed).

Find Binyamin on Twitter: @A_Binyamin

199: DREAMS

by Binyamin Bashir

Longingly, I hoped for a better tale of bright futures. I forcefully kicked off my boots and lay back bitterly on my bed. I thought bleakly of all the pressures of the twitching world. Its boastful insistence. Its hauntingly devious seduction, then destruction of those who hopelessly fight. Fate was inconsistently and ferociously damning in its strike.

I judged every failure harshly, and they all brutally responded. I breathed in painfully. My eyes filled up hatefully. Sadly, I sank into my dreams.

~

Binyamin Bashir's Biography

See story 198.

200: THE GOOD, THE BAD AND THE CHARITABLE

by Laura May

May May walked through a misty London, the swirling, clinging lowly hung clouds draping lovingly and coldly around her. There's a man sleeping in a doorway, quietly but unquestioningly shivering underneath his thinly spread blankets, a damp cardboard sign desperately propped up wonkily next to him asking for food or money, going frustratingly ignored by a busy London.

May May resolutely takes off her coat, stubbornly ignoring the abruptly stinging cold. She drapes it lovingly over the unknowing gentleman. May May walks on warmly in the quietly cold London. The gentleman later wakes up warmly in the bustlingly busy city.

~

Laura May's Biography

No author biography supplied.

A FINAL NOTE

Mike and I would like to say one last THANK YOU to all the authors featured in this anthology. Their generosity is helping support a very worthy charity and it's an honour to present their stories in this collection.

Don't forget to check my website for more writing challenges – they will be appearing regularly in the future. You will be able to find all the details here: www.christopherfielden.com/writing-challenges/

I will say farewell Bristol-style:

Cheers me dears,

Chris Fielden

17474413R00068

Printed in Poland
by Amazon Fulfillment
Poland Sp. z o.o., Wrocław